Fireman Sam™

Trouble and Squeak

One morning, Sam saw Norman carrying something covered in a blue cloth. "What have you got there?" he asked.

"This is the most daring mouse in Pontypandy!" said Norman, proudly. "He can run up a ladder, dive through the air and land in a tub of cheese spread! Meet The Great Squeakendo!"

Mandy sighed. "He's Squeaky, the school mouse," she said. "Our teacher said Norman could look after him for the holidays."

Norman and Mandy took Squeaky to Norman's bedroom. They unrolled lots of rolls of toilet paper and taped the cardboard tubes together. They had made a maze for Squeaky!

Norman put a piece of cheese at one end. "Now, The Great Squeakendo will find his way through the Maze of Mystery!" he said.

But Squeaky's cage was empty.

"Oh no!" said Norman. "He's escaped. Where is he?"

Meanwhile, Sarah and James were at Fireman Sam's house. Sam was showing the twins his latest invention.

"What is it?" Sarah asked.
"It's a grabber," he told them.
"The arms get longer so it can grab things that are too high to reach."

"Wow!" said James.

"That's really cool, Uncle Sam!' said Sarah.

Back at the shop, Dilys was having a cup of tea when Squeaky peeped out of the biscuit tin. He was nibbling one of her biscuits!

"Aaaaargh!" screamed Dilys.

Upstairs, Norman and Mandy heard the commotion outside. They looked out of the window and saw Dilys with a brush. She was sweeping Squeaky out into the street!

"Get out, you little pest!" said Dilys.

Mandy and Norman ran downstairs.

"That's not a pest, Mam,"
said Norman, as Squeaky ran
off down the street. "He's the
school pet! I'm looking after him!"

"Oh dear!" said Dilys. "I wish
you had warned me, Norman.
He was after my custard creams!"

Norman and Mandy ran off in the
direction Squeaky had run.

"He can't have
gone far,"
said Mandy.
"Don't worry,
Norman.
We'll find him."

Norman and Mandy searched everywhere for Squeaky but they couldn't find him.

They decided to make posters with Squeaky's picture on them and stick them up around the village.

First, they took one to the Fire Station. Fireman Sam had a look. "Oh, dear! Poor Squeaky, hopefully the posters will help find him," he said.

"His tail's bent and his ears stick out …" Norman told Sam.
"I have to find him."

Meanwhile, Dilys was busy working in her shop when the phone rang. It was Norman's teacher calling to ask if Squeaky, the school pet, was OK.

"Oh, he's fine," said Dilys. "Norman's … er … drawn pictures of him. Pinning them up all over town he is …"

Dilys was worried. "Oh, Norman Price, you'd better find that mouse!" Dilys said to herself.

Squeaky, meanwhile, had crept into Bella's café. He was nibbling on some cheese that Bella was about to put on Trevor's pizza!

"Ai-ai-ai!" said Bella. "A giant-a rat! He steal-a my cheese!"

"That's not a rat, it's The Great Squeakendo!" said Trevor. "His posters are all over town!"

Trevor tried to catch Squeaky, but he ran away.

Rosa chased Squeaky around the café.

"Hisssss!" said Rosa.

"Eeeek!" said Squeaky.

Just then, Norman and Mandy arrived.

"Squeaky!" cried Norman. "I thought I would never see you again!"

"Grab him!" Mandy cried.

But Squeaky was too fast for them. He ran straight up the chimney, and so did Rosa!

"Squeak!" squeaked Squeaky.

"Miaoow!" howled Rosa.

"Come down, Squeakendo,"
called Norman.

"Come-a down from-a the chimney,
Rosa," said Bella.

"It looks like they're stuck up
the chimney!"
said Trevor.

"We should call
Fireman Sam,"
said Mandy.
"He'll know
what to do."

Fireman Sam soon arrived.
He put his new grabber up the
chimney and gently grabbed Rosa.

"MIAOW!" cried Rosa.

"I've got her!" said Sam, slowly
pulling a very sooty Rosa out
of the chimney.

Once Rosa was out of the
chimney, Squeaky ran down
and Norman picked him up.

"The Great Escaping
Squeakendo!" said Norman.
"I'm taking you home!"

When Norman got back to his mum's shop, Dilys handed the phone to him. It was his teacher calling again.

"Yes, Miss," said Norman. "Squeaky's fine. We've been playing … er …"

"Squeak!"
said Squeaky suddenly.

"That's right, hide and squeak!" smiled Norman.